Angkat

The Cambodian Cinderella

written by Jewell Reinhart Coburn

illustrated by Eddie Flotte

Shen's Books

Fremont, California

To my son, Dr. William III, who trekked with me in Cambodia; and
my daughter, Ashley Jewell, for her scholarly translation of French-Khmer lore.
—J.R.C.—

To my son, Joshua, who is always in my heart; and special thanks to
Juliet Cortez, Stella Chan, Joel Suarez, and Ashlynne Quinsaat for modeling.
—E.F.—

Shen's Books
Fremont, California

(800)456-6660
http://www.shens.com

First Edition
10 9 8 7 6 5

Library of Congress Cataloging-in-Publication Data

Coburn, Jewell Reinhart.
Angkat: the Cambodian Cinderella / written by Jewell Reinhart Coburn ;
illustrated by Eddie Flotte. -- 1st ed.
[32p.]   29 cm.
Summary : A Cambodian version of Cinderella in which a poor girl marries a prince,
is killed by her jealous stepfamily, and then, through her virtue, returns to become queen.
ISBN 1-885008-09-0
[1. Fairy tales. 2. Folklore--Cambodia.] I. Flotte, Edmund, ill.
II. Cinderella. English. III. Title.
PZ8.C64An 1998   398.2'09596'02--dc21   97-35686   CIP   AC

Author's Note

My interest in exploring the folklore of Southeast Asia has taken me deep into the steaming jungles, emerald rice fields, and remote villages of Cambodia. The fascinating history and traditions of this nation have captured my interest for many years.

Khmer culture has existed in Cambodia since 4000 BC. It was the dominant force between the 9th and 13th centuries. Its art, architecture, and social systems flourished at that time and still continue as a major influence. Wreathed in jungle vines, the Temple ruins of Angkor today remain a powerful legacy of Khmer art and culture. Eddie and I have placed the story of *Angkat* (pronounced ON-kaht) against a background of beautiful landscapes and intricately carved architecture. The text and illustrations portray the unique qualities of ancient Cambodian art and life.

Angkat—child of ashes—was first found in an essay entitled *"Le Conte de Cendrillo Ches Les Cham"* written by *Adhemard Leclére,* a French folklorist who lived in Cambodia in the late 1800s. With the help and support of Mr. Riem Men, a Cambodian educator, this tale of Cinderella is adapted for the first time into the English language. In this story *Angkat* upholds the traditional Khmer values of duty, loyalty, and perseverance which are also prevalent in Cinderella's European versions.

Long, long ago in the land of Cambodia, there lived a lonely fisherman and his daughter, Angkat. Their riverside home in a quiet inlet was sheltered by waving palms. Being dutiful and obedient, Angkat was the joy of her father's life.

Beyond the fisherman's ponds there lived a widow and her daughter, Kantok. She was a girl of great beauty but had no redeeming qualities.

While cleaning his fish ponds one day the lonely fisherman and the widow met. They were soon married. The minute Angkat and Kantok became stepsisters the new wife insisted that her daughter be known as Number One daughter in the family. That was the most important of family distinctions.

Angkat protested, "But I am my father's daughter, and I am entitled to be the Number One child!" Discontentment filled the air and in no time at all, there was little peace in the new family.

The stepmother devised a plan to make her daughter Number One. Each girl would take a basket to the fish pond. The title of honor would be awarded to the daughter who returned with the biggest catch of fish.

"An easy task," Angkat thought, "I like to fish." She picked up her basket and skipped lightly down the path to the largest pond, singing to herself.

Kantok, on the other hand, was every bit as lazy as she was beautiful. She dawdled and dallied. Stopping here to watch the monkeys, stopping there to smell the blossoms of the champa trees, Kantok played all the way to the pond.

When Angkat reached the fish pond, she draped her sampot over a plumeria branch and slipped gracefully into the cool, clear water. She worked hard and before long had enticed four fish into her basket.

Kantok called out to her, "Your lips are turning blue, Angkat! You'll soon be as blue as the fish."

Cold, tired and needing to rest, Angkat wedged her fish basket between two rocks on the shore. She wrapped herself in her warm, dry sampot and lay down among the grasses and reeds. Angkat was soon fast asleep.

Having caught no fish on her own, Kantok sneaked over to Angkat's basket and stole three of her fish. She then tipped Angkat's basket so it would seem as if the missing fish had escaped on their own. Grabbing her now full basket, Kantok hurried home to claim her reward.

Angkat awoke to find her stepsister gone and her own basket containing only one fish! Now she was destined to be forever the Number Two daughter. She would have to be the family servant and could never complain.

With a heavy heart, Angkat made her way home carrying her basket with the one small fish. Feeling trapped just like the helpless fish, she released it into the smallest of her father's ponds.

The obedient Angkat took on the duties of Number Two daughter. She cleaned the house, cooked the meals, and gathered the firewood. But nothing she did pleased anyone. Stepmother and Kantok were always cruel to her, and Angkat became very sad. No longer did she greet each new day with a smile. No longer did she skip along the path or sing while she worked.

One day, as Angkat set out joylessly to work, she passed by the small pond where she had freed the little fish. To her surprise, the fish jumped high out of the water. It spun and gleamed in the shimmering presence of a mystical light, twisting and flashing its iridescent tail.

"Come to me, Angkat," the magical fish called to her.

"How beautiful you have become, Little Fish," Angkat said, realizing the presence of a good spirit. "You shall be my special friend. I'll share my rice with you every day," Angkat promised with a smile.

Angkat began saving a small portion of her rice from each meal to feed her new-found friend. With Little Fish nearby, Angkat was no longer lonely.

Kantok became suspicious of Angkat's new happiness and followed her one day. She hid among the bamboo, spying as Angkat talked to Little Fish and fed it rice from her hand. When Angkat went merrily on her way, Kantok concocted a plan.

The next morning after Angkat left to work far up the river, Kantok went straight to the small pond carrying a morsel of rice. As she reached the pond, Little Fish smelled the rice and rose to the surface. Its rainbow fins flashed in the golden sunlight. Too late to realize the danger, Little Fish was scooped into a basket. Kantok rushed home to cook it for her lunch.

When Angkat stopped to visit her tiny friend on her way home from the river, Little Fish was nowhere to be found. Overcome with grief, Angkat ran home, curled up on her mat, and wept quietly.

Suddenly she was startled by a radiating white light. Shining with kindness, the Spirit of Virtue stood before her. "I have been watching over you. I understand why your heart is broken, my child."

The Spirit gently told Angkat about the fate of her magic fish. "Tonight, place the fish bones under your mat. In the morning a surprise will await you."

After giving further instructions the Spirit faded away. Angkat found the bones in the kitchen and hastily hid them under her mat.

As dawn broke over her riverside home, Angkat was astonished to find the fish bones gone. Two dainty, golden slippers had taken their place. Angkat, although puzzled, carefully followed the Spirit's advice. "At night, leave one slipper hidden under your mat," he had said. "Put the other one by your open window."

Just as the rising sun shone through the morning mist, Angkat awoke to a great flapping of wings. She sat bolt upright. A huge, black bird was at her window. In a flash, it snatched up the one slipper and flew away, high over the palms.

"Come back," cried Angkat, running to the window. But the big, black bird was already out of sight.

Meanwhile, strolling through the lush gardens in the courtyard of the palace, the king's son saw a mystical bird hovering above. With a sudden swoop, it opened its giant beak and dropped the golden slipper into the Prince's hands.

The young Crown Prince wondered, "Why would so delicate a slipper be dropped here?"

An excited buzz grew throughout the court as the Prince summoned his courtiers. In a determined voice he announced, "Tell every young woman of the land to come and try on this golden slipper. Plan a celebration, and the maiden whose foot this slipper fits shall be my bride."

"Surely you don't expect to try on the Prince's slipper," Stepmother growled at Angkat as she was dressing to go to the palace. "You have too much work to do!"

Stepmother took a large bowl of rice and scattered it over the nearby field. She sneered at Angkat, "Of course, you are welcome to attend the celebration. That is, after you have collected every single grain of rice." With that, Kantok, Stepmother, and Father left for the palace.

Angkat set about the impossible task of gathering all the rice, when magically around her feet a flock of chickens appeared. Angkat watched in amazement. Her feathered friends pecked in the grass, cackling all the while. Before long they had filled her basket with every grain of rice.

Thanking the chickens, Angkat scampered home. She ran inside the house to change her clothes. In her best sarong, with the other beautiful slipper hidden inside, she set off for the palace.

When Angkat reached the palace gate, the Prince was pleased to see her because he had tried the golden slipper on every other girl in the kingdom.

He pointed at Angkat saying, "Come here quickly." Then he ordered his courtiers, "Unfold the carpet for this maiden to try on the slipper."

Timidly, Angkat stepped forward. She slipped her small foot gracefully into the tiny golden shoe. She reached inside her sarong and pulled out the other slipper. A great gasp arose throughout the palace grounds.

At once, the Prince understood the reason for his search. His eyes softened and with a loving look, he whispered to Angkat, "It is destiny that we should meet." He proclaimed to the crowd gathered at the palace, "My search is over. I have found my bride."

To a chorus of cheers, the Prince summoned the court ladies who welcomed the village girl into the palace. With fragrant oils, fine silk, and a multitude of flowers, they turned her into a princess.

The Prince and Angkat were soon married and became a very happy couple. However, Angkat's happiness was not to last for long.

Angkat's stepmother, stepsister, and even her own father were consumed with jealousy. They hatched a plan.

"We'll do away with Angkat," Stepmother said with a menacing jeer, "and we'll see to it that Kantok takes her place."

A few weeks later, the fisherman sent a letter to the palace. He wrote, "I am gravely ill, dear Honorable One. If it pleases you, kindly grant permission for my daughter to return home. I am in great need of her."

Because the Prince loved Angkat very much, he granted her father's request. But the minute she arrived home, the Princess was put to work. "Hot soup will make your father well," ordered Stepmother. "You know how he likes it. You make the soup!"

Outside the house, the fire roared and the great iron soup pot came to a boil. When Angkat leaned down to add more wood to the cooking fire, her cruel stepmother gave the signal, "Now!" Together, the scheming threesome pushed with all their might. Over went the cauldron on top of Angkat. The Princess was crushed and died instantly.

The wicked ones conspired together, "Our chance has finally come!"

They put on sorrowful faces and appeared before the Prince to give him the tragic news.

"Oh, Honorable One, we are grief-stricken by the death of Angkat." Then they hastily shoved Kantok before the Prince. "Be assured, though, that you will not be without a wife."

The kindhearted Prince, not wishing to dishonor the memory of his treasured young bride, agreed to allow Kantok to live in the palace.

Returning home, Stepmother and Father found an unusual surprise. At the very place where Angkat had been killed, a beautiful red-leafed banana plant had mysteriously appeared, its leaves glossy and broad.

"That plant was not here yesterday. Where did it come from?" asked Stepmother, alarmed and frightened. "Do something!" she cried, fearful that Angkat's spirit had come back to haunt them.

"I'll get rid of it," Father agreed. He ran for his machete and hacked the banana plant to pieces. He hoisted the stalk and leaves onto his shoulders and made his way deep into the forest. As Father threw down the banana plant pieces, sturdy bamboo shoots rose out of the ground. A massive stand of graceful bamboo appeared, gently waving in the breeze. The wicked fisherman was amazed and bewildered.

Needless to say, the heartbroken Prince continued to mourn the untimely death of his cherished wife. One day, to ease the sorrow, his companions decided to take him hunting. Together, they all set out for the jungle.

They forded swift streams. They trekked through dense forests. Tired at last, the hunting party agreed to set up camp and rest under a majestic grove of bamboo.

"Is this a dream?" thought the Prince. But no, he heard it again, a soft, rustling sound. Entranced, the Prince listened intently. So pure and gentle was the sound of the evening breeze through the bamboo that the Prince grieved all the more for Angkat, his lost love.

"What I was hunting for, I may have found. I must have this bamboo at my palace. Dig it up!" He insisted.

Instead of jungle kills, the Prince's astonished companions trudged back to the palace, weighted down with bundles of bamboo.

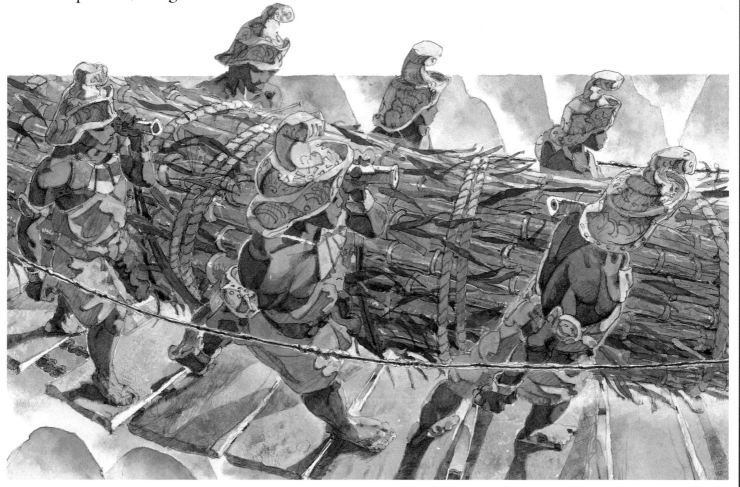

Day after day, the Prince sat alone in the cool, green shade of his bamboo grove. One day he heard the peculiar sound again and listened more closely. Softer than a breath, he heard Angkat's voice whispering in the bamboo, "I am here with you, my dear Prince."

Falling to his knees, the Prince beseeched the Spirit of Virtue for the return of his one true love.

Suddenly he felt a presence, faintly at first. He looked up. In the pale green bamboo surrounded by a shining light, stood his cherished Angkat glowing with inner beauty. The Prince reached out to his beloved Princess. Their hands touched and they felt blessed by the Spirit.

Peering from her window at this scene, Kantok shrieked. In panic she fled from the palace pursued by cats hissing, dogs howling, and birds fluttering wildly. Together with the cruel, scheming stepmother and father, the three were banished forever from the land.

The Prince was crowned King and Angkat became his rightful Queen. Rising above their tragedies, they brought prosperity and happiness to the people. From that day forth the Spirit of Virtue blessed them abundantly. Peace and joy reigned over the magnificent kingdom of Cambodia for many years to come.

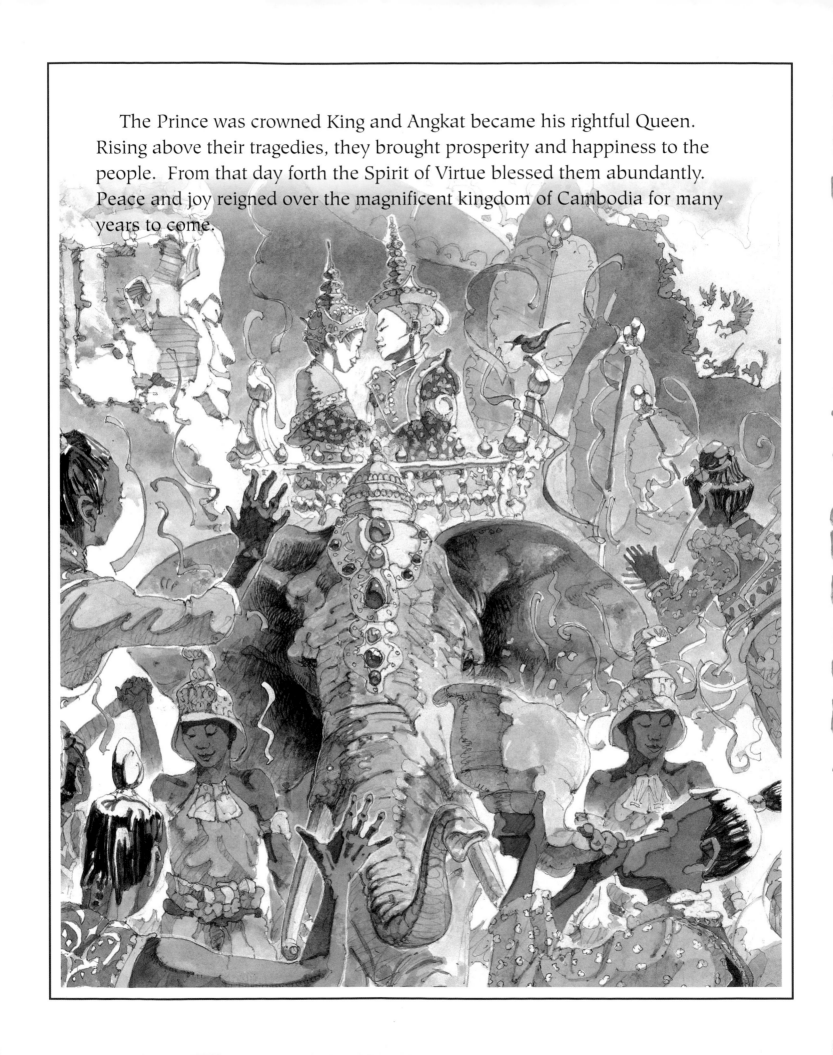